To Georgia M. —A.G.

For Imogen —P.M.

Text ©1997 by Anne Gatti
Illustrations ©1997 by Peter Malone

Conceived by The Artworks Press.
Book design by Vandy Ritter.
Typeset in Centaur MT and Ovidius.
Printed in Hong Kong.

Library of Congress Cataloging-in-Publication Data
Gatti, Anne
The magic flute / retold by Anne Gatti; illustrated by Peter Malone
p. cm.
Summary: Retells the story of the Mozart opera in which the noble Prince Tamino
saves the fair Pamina against a backdrop of the battle between darkness and light.
ISBN: 0-8118-1003-8
1. Mozart, Wolfgang Amadeus, 1756-1791 Zauberflöte. 2. Operas—Stories, plots, etc.
[1. Operas—Stories, plots, etc.] 1756-1791. Zauberflöte. III. Title.
MT100. M8G37 1997
782.1í02669—dc21   97-1348
                                                    CIP
                                                    M AC

Distributed in Canada by Raincoast Books
8680 Cambie Street
Vancouver B.C. V6P 6M9

10 9 8 7 6 5 4 3 2

Chronicle Books
85 Second Street
San Francisco, CA 94105

Website: www.chronbooks.com

The Magic Flute

Retold by Anne Gatti

Illustrated by Peter Malone

chronicle books · san francisco

Musical Selections

Following are the musical highlights from *The Magic Flute* that are included on the enclosed compact disc. The listing below contains: the title of each selection, the length of playing time, the scene where the selection occurs within the story, and a brief summary.

1. *Overture*; 7:30
from the scene "The Prince and the Monster"

2. *I am the Birdcatcher (Der Vogelfänger bin ich ja)* sung by Papageno; 2:45
from the scene "The Birdman"
Papageno introduces himself to Tamino.

3. *This portrait is bewitching (Dies Bildnis ist bezaubernd schön)* sung by Tamino; 4:00
from the scene "Queen of the Night"
Tamino is mesmerized by the picture of Pamina.

4. *Hm! hm! hm! hm!* sung by Papageno, Tamino, and all three ladies; 5:06
from the scene "Queen of the Night"
The ladies of the forest place a lock on Papageno's mouth and he cannot talk.

5. *A man who can feel love must have a good heart (Bei männern, welche liebe fuhlen)* sung by Pamina and Papageno; 3:11
from the scene "The Captive Princess"
Pamina asks Papageno about the prince Tamino.

6. *How powerful is your magic music! (Wie stark ist nicht dein Zauberton!)* sung by Tamino; 3:05
from the scene "The Prince's Magic Flute"
At Sorastro's temple, Tamino plays his magic flute and all the wild animals gather peacefully around him.

7. *Swift feet and ready courage (Schnelle Fuße rascher mut)* sung by Pamina, Papageno and Monostatos; 1:40
from the scene "The Wise Ruler"
Papageno and Pamina hope that speed and courage will protect them from danger in the temple, but Monostatos catches them.

8. Act II *March of the Priests (Marsch der Priester)*; 2:42
from the scene "The First Trial"
Tamino enters the Temple of Wisdom.

9. *O Isis and Osiris (O isis und Osiris)* sung by Sorastro and Chorus; 2:52
from the scene "The First Trial"
As Pamina and Tamino enter the temple, Sorastro asks the gods to grant them wisdom and strength.

10. *Vengeance seethes in my heart (Der Hölle Rache)* sung by the Queen; 2:49
from the scene "The Queen's Command"
The Queen asks Pamina to kill Sorastro and get his powerful seals. As Pamina tries to say no, the Queen sings of vengeance.

11. *Ah, I feel that the joy of love has gone for evermore (Ach, ich fühl's)* sung by Pamina; 4:11
from the scene "The Prince's Dilemma"
Tamino has been sworn to silence. When Pamina finds him and he doesn't respond to her, Pamina thinks that he no longer loves her. Pamina is heartbroken.

12. *A Sweetheart or a Wife (Ein Mädchen oder Weibchen)* sung by Papageno; 4:08
from the scene "The Promise"
Papageno realizes that what he really wants is a mate.

13. *My Tamino! Oh, what happiness! (Tamino mein! O welch ein Glück)* sung by Pamina 4:10
from the scene "The Second Trial"
Tamino and Pamina are reunited in front of the furnace of flames. Pamina is delighted to see Tamino again.

14. *Papagena! Papagena! Papagena;* sung by Papageno; 5:42
from the scene "The Flying Machine"
Papageno sings about Papagena, the mate, he wants to find.

15. *Papagena!...Papageno!* sung by Papageno and Papagena; 2:32
from the scene "The Third Trial"
Papageno and Papagena are happily reunited.

16. *The rays of the sun chase night away! (Die Strahlen der Sonne...Heil sei euch Geweihten!)* sung by Sorastro and Chorus; 2:55
from the scene "The Celebration"
Tamino and Pamina stand before Sorastro at the temple. Sorastro sings of the goodness that has prevailed and the bright rays of the sun that have chased the darkness away.

Mozart and the Magic Flute

Born in Salzburg, Austria in 1756, Wolfgang Amadeus Mozart is arguably the greatest composer of our time. A child prodigy, he began composing before the age of five, and by the age of thirteen he had written concertos, sonatas, symphonies and an operetta.

His most famous works include *The Marriage of Figaro* (1786), an opera which inspired the citizens of Vienna to whistle Figaro's arias in the streets, and *Don Giovanni* (1787), considered to be one of the most brilliant operas ever written. Mozart's music is known the world over for its classical grace, its passion and technical perfection.

However, for much of his life Mozart struggled to make a living. Of a passionate and, some believe, a disquieted mind, Mozart despised the system of servitude which dictated his life and his art. He was a man ahead of his time. Only a few of his masterpieces were hailed as such during his lifetime. Except for his good friend and fellow composer, Joseph Haydn, many of Mozart's contemporaries did not understand his music, just as they did not understand the man who created it. At the age of thirty-five, Mozart died penniless and was buried in an unmarked pauper's grave.

In 1791, the year he died, Mozart wrote *The Magic Flute*. One of his most popular operas, it was Mozart's first work created for the popular theater rather than under the patronage of the royalty or nobility. A "magic opera," *The Magic Flute* is a fairy tale. Indeed, many of the elements of the opera come from legends, folktales and classical comedy. A magical world of flying machines, butterflies the size of birds, and a pair of perfect lovers, Mozart's opera is also an allegory, imbued with a deep belief in the triumph of good over evil.

The Prince and the Monster

One day a handsome prince named Tamino went out hunting. Tracking wild animals, he stalked his way across his father's kingdom until he found himself in a strange, rocky land. Tamino had been concentrating so hard on following his quarry that he had not noticed he had strayed so far. Nor had he noticed the fading daylight. Now, as the sky grew dark, he peered into the gloom to see if he could find shelter for the night.

Suddenly, there was a loud crackling noise behind him. Tamino spun around. There, only a leap away, was a horrible monster. It had the body of a man but the head of a snake. Its eyes burned an evil yellow and its forked tongue darted in and out of its mouth with a terrible hissing sound.

Terrified, Tamino sprinted away with the speed of a hare, shouting, "Help! Help!" at the top of his voice. But the faster he ran, the closer the hissing came. Tamino tried to dodge behind some rocks but stumbled and fell, knocking his head on a stone. As the monster lunged toward the prince, three dark-haired ladies suddenly appeared, armed with shining spears and swords. With one swift movement, all three plunged their weapons into the monster's side. It let out a deafening roar and crumpled to the ground, stone dead.

The three ladies retrieved their weapons and then peered closely at the sleeping prince.

"I never saw such a fair face," said one.

"I'll guard him while you two report to the queen," suggested another.

"No, no. I'll keep watch over him. You two go," insisted the third.

In the end, they couldn't agree on who should stay, so all three hurried away to tell their queen, the ruler of this rocky land, about the mysterious stranger.

 Selection 1

The Birdman

A few minutes later, Tamino began to stir. He rubbed his sore head and sat up, trying to remember where he was. When he saw the monster's blood-stained body he leaped backwards in fright. But then realized that the monster was dead and began to look around to see who had killed it. As he did so, he heard the sound of panpipes floating from the nearby trees, and a man's voice singing. Then out skipped a wiry figure, with a beaky nose and feathers in his hair. He was carrying a basket on his back.

"Who are you?" shouted the prince in alarm.

"Silly question. A man, of course," came the reply. Then the skipping stranger came closer and explained that he caught birds for the Queen of the Night and was given food and drink in return.

"Is it you I must thank for killing this monster?" Tamino asked him.

"Think nothing of it," chirped the birdman as he hopped from foot to foot.

"But you have no weapons. How did you do it?"

"Oh! Brute strength," bragged the birdman. "I…"

But his boast was cut short by an angry shout of "PAPAGENO!" Tamino turned around to see the three dark-haired ladies standing behind him. The birdman made a strange, clucking noise and quickly handed the ladies a bird from his basket. But instead of the wine and cake he was expecting, they gave him water and a stone. Then one of them brought her hand up to his mouth.

"And now, I have the pleasure of closing your lying mouth with this," she said, snapping a padlock onto his lips.

Papageno hopped up and down indignantly, trying to speak, but the ladies ignored him. They walked over to the astonished Tamino and handed him a picture of a beautiful girl. But before Tamino could ask a single question, they vanished.

 Selection 2

Queen of the Night

Tamino stood gazing at the picture and knew instantly that he was in love. Papageno tugged again and again at Tamino's sleeve, pointing to his padlocked lips, but the prince did not even seem to notice him. Suddenly there was a clap of thunder and the sky turned inky black. Tamino, who had been shaken out of his daydream, shielded his eyes as a flash of lightning lit up the ground. He felt a sudden gust of icy cold wind and then saw that there was a black-haired lady with steely-gray eyes and a long, dark cloak standing in front of him.

"I am the Queen of the Night," she announced. "It is my daughter Pamina whom you've been admiring. She was snatched from me by the evil sorcerer Sorastro, and I shall never be able to rest until she is rescued. If you bring her back to me, I will let you marry her."

Tamino stared at the queen and then glanced down at the sweet face in the picture. He must rescue the princess, that was certain. But should he trust this cold-eyed queen? He shivered as he felt a blast of icy wind once more. Then daylight returned and he saw that in the queen's place stood the three ladies who were unfastening Papageno's padlock.

"I promise I'll never tell a single lie again!" Papageno blurted out as soon as he could speak.

"Good!" replied the ladies. "Now, listen to the queen's command: you are to take Prince Tamino to Sorastro's secret temple."

"Cheep! Cheep! Can you hear those birds? I'm sorry, ladies, but I must run and catch them because you see they're very rare and…"

"Here is a box of magic bells," continued the ladies, ignoring Papageno's excuses. "They will help you should you find yourself in trouble."

Then they approached Tamino. "And for you, Prince, we have this magic flute. Farewell!"

"Wait!" shouted Papageno as they turned to go. "I don't know the way. I need a map."

"Don't worry," they replied. "There are three young boys on the edge of Sorastro's kingdom. They will guide you." The next moment, the three ladies vanished, and the prince and Papageno were left alone.

 Selection 3

 Selection 4

The Captive Princess

For a while Tamino and Papageno stood arguing about which way to go. In the end, they decided to split up and to call to each other with their musical instruments if one of them found the three boys.

As Papageno threaded his way through the trees, he heard a scream. He tiptoed toward the noise and found himself in a clearing. In front of him stood a magnificent castle. Papageno crept up to an open doorway and peered in. There he saw a beautiful girl who was being tied to a pillar by an evil-looking man. Papageno was so frightened he let out a squawk and the man spun around angrily. Papageno could feel his feathers trembling but when the man saw the birdman he dropped the rope and ran from the room.

Papageno patted his feathers to calm himself and went to untie the girl. He studied her for a moment and then pulled out the picture Tamino had given him.

"Mmm! Long brown hair. Yes. Dark eyes. Yes. Red lips. Yes. Everything matches, except for your feet and hands. According to your picture, you haven't any!"

"What do you mean?" asked the confused girl. "Who are you?"

"I'm Papageno and I work for the Queen of the Night. She has sent myself and a prince to rescue you – that's if you're Pamina. Are you?"

"Yes, yes I am. I was trying to run away from Sorastro but I was followed by his cruel chancellor, Monostatos, who caught me and…" She stopped and then, as if she'd suddenly remembered something more important, asked, "Who is this prince you spoke of?"

"He arrived in your mother's kingdom today. She gave him a picture of you and asked him to rescue you. He's already fallen in love with you, and so he agreed."

"Fallen in love?" repeated the princess, blushing. "Where is he?"

"That's the only problem," answered Papageno. "I've lost him."

 Selection 5

The Prince's Magic Flute

While Papageno was rescuing the princess, Tamino found the three boys who took him to a tall building with sturdy pillars and three vast entrances. As they arrived, one of the boys explained, "This is Sorastro's temple. You'll find what you're seeking here, but you must be patient and brave." Then the three guides waved farewell and walked away through the trees.

Tamino was on his own once more. He decided to try one of the enormous doors, but as he pushed against the one on the right, a thunderous voice called out, "Go back!"

Tamino was so determined to find Pamina that he crossed to the left-hand door and pushed again with all his might. "Go back!" rang the same voice.

Still Tamino did not give up. He stood in front of the middle door and raised his fist to hammer on it when, to his surprise, the door swung open and out came an old man in long robes, his hands held crossed in front of him.

"What do you want, stranger?" he asked.

"I have come to rescue Princess Pamina from the wicked sorcerer Sorastro."

"Sorastro is no sorcerer, but a wise ruler."

"But didn't he steal Pamina from her mother?"

"That is true. But it is not for you to question the ways of the wise."

The old man turned around and went back into the building. The door closed with a thud.

"Is Pamina still alive?" shouted Tamino after him.

"Yes…yes…yes…," echoed a deep voice from inside the temple.

Tamino was happy to hear that Pamina was alive, but he was puzzled about what to do next. He decided to look for Papageno and so he pulled the flute out of his belt and put it to his lips. As soon as the notes filled the air, a host of animals came from the depths of the forest and formed a circle around him.

Tamino was astonished at how tame they seemed but he continued to play. After a few minutes he heard the high, clear notes of Papageno's panpipes, and he ran to meet his companion.

 Selection 6

The Wise Ruler

Pamina and Papageno, who had heard Tamino's flute, were also running through the trees. "This way," panted Pamina, "hurry."

"Hurry!" sneered a voice behind them. They turned around and found themselves face to face with Monostatos, Sorastro's chancellor. Behind him stood several of his servants carrying coils of rope. Pamina cried out to Papageno for help, but the birdman, who was trembling with fear, looked blankly at her. Then he remembered what the three ladies had said about finding himself in trouble. He delved into his pocket and pulled out the box of bells.

"Ring, little bells, ring, and send them into a spin," he whispered as he opened the box and began to play. Instantly Monostatos and his servants started to spin wildly like dancers at a wedding feast. Pamina and Papageno could hardly believe their luck and tore off through the trees once more. The hadn't gone far when they heard a fanfare of trumpets.

"Oh no!" cried Pamina. "It's Sorastro."

Ahead they could see a wide path and the tall figure of Sorastro, dressed in golden robes, standing in his chariot. Papageno hid behind a tree, but Pamina approached, dropped to her knees and begged for forgiveness.

"Sir, I know I tried to run away but Monostatos tied me up and I was afraid of what he might do to me."

Sorastro took Pamina's hand and gently helped her to her feet.

"I know you are good," he said, "and as you will discover, I only want what is good for you. I did not know that wicked servant of mine had imprisoned you. He shall certainly be punished for his cruelty."

"Oh, Sire, why can't I return to my mother?" pleaded Pamina.

"Trust me," replied Sorastro. "You will soon know why it is better that you do not go back to her."

Just then there was a loud snapping of twigs and Pamina turned to see Monostatos emerging from the trees. He was dragging a stranger who was clutching a flute. Instantly she knew that this handsome man was the prince Tamino, who had come to rescue her. She ran towards him, and like a pair of long-lost friends, they embraced.

 Selection 7

The First Trial

"Sire." Monostatos shouted angrily. "Arrest this man and punish him! He's come to steal Pamina from your kingdom."

"Yes," replied Sorastro, "punishment is a good idea. But not for him." He pointed an accusing finger at Monostatos. "For you! Guards, take him away."

Papageno, who had been watching everything from behind his tree, now stepped out. No sooner had he greeted the prince and princess than they were interrupted by Sorastro.

"Welcome to our kingdom," he said, holding out his hand to Tamino. "I can see that you have love in your heart, but before you can win your heart's desire, you must first prove yourself worthy. To do this, you and your companion must enter our temple." With that he signaled to the guards and, before Papageno could protest, he and Tamino were taken by the arm and led away. Tamino was prepared to do anything to win Pamina and so he did not complain. But Papageno, who was by now very hungry and thirsty, pestered the guards with questions about when they would give him something to eat. The guards did not answer him, but guided them through a side entrance of the temple, up a steep hill, and through a scratchy thicket until they reached level ground. The guards stopped and Papageno and Tamino found themselves in a dark courtyard. A tall man was approaching, carrying a flaming torch. Tamino recognized him as the old man who had earlier opened the door.

"Are you ready to prove yourself worthy of true love?" he asked them.

"I am," replied Tamino.

"Even if it costs you your life?"

"I am," said the prince once again.

"Now hold on," interrupted Papageno. "I don't want to prove anything! I'll be quite happy with a three-course meal, a good night's sleep...oh yes, and a pretty wife."

"You'll never get one unless you take part in the trials that we have set for you," insisted the old man.

"In that case, I'll stay single." answered Papageno.

"Even if Sorastro has a young and beautiful girl waiting for you?"

"What's her name?" asked Papageno.

"Papagena."

"Mmm! I wouldn't mind taking a look at her..."

"But you must agree to remain silent until we give

you permission to talk. You, too, Tamino. This is your first trial."

The prince and Papageno nodded in agreement and the old man walked away into the darkness. Papageno sat on a stone bench feeling very sorry for himself. I wish I was back in my woods, listening to my birds, he thought. Keeping silent is thirsty work and there doesn't seem to be even a beakful of water around. Suddenly, he heard footsteps and looked up. An old woman was hobbling by, carrying a jug.

"Hey! You!" he called, forgetting his promise to keep silent. "Can I have a drink?"

The old woman offered him some of her water and he took a long drink.

"How old are you?" he asked.

"Eighteen years and two minutes," she replied.

Papageno burst out laughing. Then he asked, "Do you have a boyfriend?"

"Of course."

"And what's he called?"

"Papageno."

"Papageno!" he sputtered. "And what's…your …name?"

But before the old woman could answer, there was a deafening roll of thunder and she was gone.

Selection 8

Selection 9

The Queen's Command

Outside the temple walls, Pamina, who had been waiting for Tamino to reappear, had fallen asleep. When she awoke, shivering with the cold, she found her mother towering above her, her dark cloak just visible against the black sky. Without even greeting her daughter, the Queen of the Night snapped, "Where is the prince I sent to rescue you?"

Pamina, who was delighted to see her mother but also nervous of her temper, explained, "Sorastro says Tamino must prove himself worthy of love and so he has sent him to the temple. Oh, Mother, I don't know what to do! Please protect me."

"Protect you?" scoffed the queen. "I can't protect you unless you bring me the seal of the seven circles of the sun which your father foolishly gave to Sorastro before he died. Without this seal, I have no powers. Here," she said, pulling out a dagger from under her dark cloak and thrusting it into Pamina's hand, "you must kill Sorastro and bring me back the magic seal."

Pamina drew back, horrified at the thought of killing the man whom she now knew to be kind and wise.

Just then, a gust of icy wind blew the queen's veil across her face, and she vanished.

Pamina paced up and down, close to tears. She loved Tamino, that was certain. And she trusted Sorastro. She felt she ought to love her mother, but how could she, after she had just asked her to kill Sorastro? Lost in her thoughts, she did not notice Sorastro approaching her. She looked up, saw him, and dropped the dagger as if it was on fire.

"Sire, please don't punish my mother," she pleaded. I'm sure she doesn't mean any harm."

Sorastro looked kindly at Pamina. "She wants revenge because your father gave the seven circles of the sun to me and not to her," he explained. "She is powerless without it, but would do nothing but harm if it was hers. We do not rule by hatred and revenge in this kingdom. For that reason, I forgive your mother. Now, it is time for you to rest. Come."

Pamina took Sorastro's hand and they set off toward the castle.

 Selection 10

The Prince's Dilemma

While Pamina was resting, the old man appeared once more to Tamino and Papageno, and led them through a creaking door into an echoing room.

"When you hear our trumpets you must follow their call," he explained. "And don't forget, you are still bound to silence. Farewell."

Tamino and Papageno blinked as they looked around them. They were standing in a vast, bright hall. In the center was a banquet table which was piled high with food and drink.

"Now this is more like it," said Papageno, as he started to help himself to some bread and meat. But Tamino, who was beginning to wonder if he would ever see Pamina again, did not eat a crumb. Instead, he picked up his flute. He had played only a few, sad notes when the door opened and in ran Pamina.

"Oh Tamino! At last I've found you," she exclaimed.

"But you look unhappy. Aren't you pleased to see me?"

Tamino, still bound by silence, sighed and placed a finger to his lips.

"Why won't you talk to me?" cried Pamina.

Tamino shook his head.

"Don't you love me?" she quavered, her eyes welling with tears.

Tamino, who couldn't bear to see Pamina's distress, turned his back to her. She glanced at Papageno for an explanation, but he had his mouth stuffed and just shrugged his shoulder. With a loud sob, Pamina ran from the room.

"See!" said Papageno cheerfully, "I can stay quiet when I want to!"

A trumpet blast interrupted his chatter and Tamino signaled to Papageno that they should follow it.

 Selection 11

The Promise

Tamino strode out of the banquet hall into a gloomy corridor. After a while the corridor divided and Tamino chose the path to the right where, in the distance, he could see the glinting handle of a door. When he reached the door, he turned the handle and found himself in a narrow tunnel which was sealed with yet another door. He tried this one too and when it opened he stepped into a low-ceilinged room. There stood Sorastro and the old man.

"Well done, Tamino," said Sorastro. "You have shown great courage and strength and you have passed the trial of silence. But before you can claim your true love, you must face two more trials."

The door opened and Pamina was ushered in. She hesitated, unsure whether she should approach Tamino. But Tamino held out his hand to her and gently said, "Pamina, I must go and prove myself worthy of you. Trust me. Our love will give me strength."

Pamina was overjoyed when she realized Tamino still loved her, but she feared for his safety. "Must you really go?" she asked.

"He must," replied Sorastro. "Now, Tamino, take your leave."

The old man waited until the prince and princess had embraced and then led Tamino out of the room.

While Tamino was preparing to undergo his second trial, Papageno was still trying to catch up with the prince. Although he had intended to follow Tamino, he could not resist running back to the banquet hall for a last handful of grapes and so he had not seen which path Tamino took. Now he stumbled along, nervously calling out for Tamino. When he reached the fork in the corridor, he too chose to go to the right. He turned the glinting handle of the first door, but when he arrived at the second door, he was thrown back by a scorching barrier of flames which erupted at his feet. He ran back to the first door but it, too, burst into flames. Papageno was frantic. There seemed to be no escape.

The next minute the old man was standing beside him and the flames had died down. "Papageno," he said. "You are not strong like the prince, and you are not as wise."

"Well," explained Papageno, who was fed up at the thought of yet more trials, "some people prefer wine to wisdom, and I happen to be one of them."

"Is that all you really want from life?" asked the old man.

Papageno nodded and in the blink of an eye the old man disappeared and in his place stood a large goblet of wine. Papageno bent down and slurped it up like a parched camel. He began to feel cheerful again and took out his bells and started to play. Now all I need, he thought, is a pretty little dove to be my wife.

Just then the old woman who had given him a drink in the courtyard came hobbling along the tunnel.

"Here I am," she cackled. "And when you agree to marry me, you'll see what a sweet wife I'll be."

"Not so fast! I'm not quite so sure I want to get married yet," squawked Papageno, as he stared at her warty skin.

"I wouldn't wait too long, otherwise you might spend the rest of your days in this dark tunnel."

When Papageno heard this he quickly changed his mind.

"Promise you will marry me?" asked the old woman.

"I promise," Papageno assured her, and as he spoke the old woman's wrinkled face melted into the smooth face of a beautiful young girl. "Pa-pa-papagena!" he exclaimed in delight. But before the girl could answer him, the old man had reappeared and stood between them.

"Come," he said sternly as he took the girl by the arm and led her down the tunnel. "This birdman is still not worthy of you."

Papageno stared in disbelief as the pair vanished into the gloom. "My dove! Flown away! But I'll find you again. Nothing will stop me, not even if the earth tries to swallow me up!"

As he spoke, Papageno felt the ground give way beneath his feet. "Oh no!" he moaned and clung tightly to his box of bells, as he tumbled into a hole.

 Selection 12

The Second Trial

Separated from her prince once more, Pamina couldn't help feeling miserable. She was wandering around a garden inside the temple when she met the three boys who had first guided Tamino through the forest. She begged them to take her to Tamino, wherever he was. The boys led her to a high, rocky place and pointed to two peaked mountains. "That's where you'll find him," they said. Then they turned and left.

Pamina ran on, calling out Tamino's name. As she approached the base of the mountains, she saw that a huge door, made of metal bars, had been cut into the side of each mountain. Through one she could see a glowing furnace of flames, through the other a misty torrent of water. Just then she spotted Tamino, flanked by two guards, walking toward the mountain of fire. She called out and he ran to greet her.

"Oh, Tamino! Take me with you!" she cried.

"I want to be with you, even if the fire burns us, or the water drowns us."

"Oh, my Pamina!" cried Tamino, as he kissed her.

"Don't forget your magic flute," she told him. "It was made by my father and will protect us on our journey."

The guards opened the metal gate in front of them and signaled to Tamino and Pamina to follow the cinder path that led deep into the mountain. As they walked forward, a wall of flames blazed on either side of them, meeting above their heads like an arch. The air was so hot that it hurt them to breathe. Sweat trickled down their foreheads into their eyes, making it difficult for them to see.

As Tamino played his flute, the searing heat became less intense and the crackle of the flames was replaced by a thunderous roar. Gradually the path sloped down. It was leading them into the mountain of water.

 Selection 13

The Flying Machine

Outside the mountain, Papageno had fallen into a large garden. He didn't know where he was, but was greatly relieved to be out of the tunnel. He leaped up and started to search for Papagena.

"Papagena! Papagena!" he shouted, but all he could hear was the echo of his own voice. "It's no good. I just couldn't keep my mouth shut, could I? And now she's gone. Life's not worth living."

He listened, his head on one side, hoping to hear the rustle of a skirt. But there was only silence. He stared at the ground miserably but then something made him look up and there, silently floating down toward the ground, was a magical flying machine covered with golden decorations that glinted in the sun. As it landed, the three boys climbed out and greeted the astonished Papageno.

"Oh Papageno!" they cried. "Don't look so gloomy. Have you forgotten about your bells? Why don't you ring them and see what happens?" And they smiled at each other as Papageno, who had clearly forgotten all about his bells, grabbed his box and started to play.

Standing with his back to the machine, Papageno picked out a lilting tune. But after a short while he stopped, disappointed that nothing had happened.

"Now, why don't you turn around?" suggested the boys.

Papageno spun around and saw his beloved Papagena, daintily stepping out of the machine. "Pa-pa-pa-pa-pa-pa-Papagena!" he stammered with delight. "Pa-pa-pa-pa-pa-pa-Papageno!" she exclaimed with joy and they fell into each other's arms.

 Selection 14

The Third Trial

While Papageno and Papagena were happily reunited, Tamino and Pamina were still braving the mountain of water. The mist was so thick that they could barely make out the path in front of them. But with every step they took, they could hear the roar of the waterfall growing louder and louder. Soon their clothes were drenched with icy spray and the noise was so deafening they could not hear each other speak. Then the path ended abruptly, blocked by a vast wall of tumbling water.

Tamino and Pamina looked up at the torrent and shivered. Pamina signaled to Tamino to try his flute. He had only played a few notes when all at once a narrow gap appeared in the middle of the waterfall. Tamino led the way along this cold, slippery track which climbed steeply, through the swirling mist, until they reached a heavy, gilded door. Together, they pushed it open and stood in the doorway, speechless at the magnificent sight in front of them: a glittering hall, lit by bright sunshine which streamed through seven circular windows. At the far end of the hall was another gilded door and in the center stood a golden throne where Sorastro was seated. Sorastro stood up and stretched out his arms toward the exhausted prince and princess.

"Welcome to our most sacred chamber in the heart of the Temple of Wisdom," he said. "Your courage and your love have been truly tested and they have held firm. Now it is time for us all to celebrate!"

Tamino turned to Pamina and took her hand. "Our trials are over. We have left the cold darkness behind forever. Come, let's walk in the light."

 Selection 15

Revenge!

Tamino and Pamina were so delighted to have survived the trials together that they had quite forgotten the Queen of the Night. The Queen, however, had not forgotten them, and when she found Monostatos skulking in the forest, she offered to give him Pamina as his wife if he would show her a safe route to the sacred chamber where she hoped to find, and steal, the seal.

"I'll help you all right," growled Monostatos. "I'll do anything you ask, as long as I get Pamina for keeps."

Then, armed with a sword and carrying a flaming torch, he led the queen and the three ladies though a dark tunnel toward the secret chamber. As they emerged onto a wide, grassy space, they could see the gilded door of the chamber.

"Now, don't forget your promise to me," snapped Monostatos. "My services in exchange for your daughter."

"Yes, yes," hissed the queen. "As soon as I lay my hands on the seal, you can have the wretched girl."

Then she turned to the ladies. "Draw your swords," she commanded. "The kingdom of the night must win back its power."

With that, thunder shook the ground and an icy blast of wind blew with such force that the chamber door swung open. Sorastro, Tamino and Pamina, framed in an arc of golden sunlight, stepped out. The light was so dazzling that the queen, Monostatos, and the ladies were all blinded and stood rooted to the spot. They lifted their arms to shield their eyes, but as they did so, the ground opened beneath them and they were hurled down into the dark earth. Struggling and shrieking they fell, deeper and deeper, until all that could be heard was a faint echo of their cries.

The Celebration

Tamino and Pamina stared in amazement as the dark hole closed over, leaving no trace of where the intruders had stood. Pamina gave a little shudder but, as soon as she felt Sorastro's strong arm around her shoulders, she understood why he had brought her to his kingdom.

"My people," Sorastro called out as his followers streamed out of the chamber and gathered around. "Our light has destroyed the evil deeds of those who live in the kingdom of darkness. And through this good pair, and the courage and strength of their love, we celebrate a new dawn that heralds a time of peace and harmony."

The people clapped and cheered, bells pealed and a fanfare of trumpets was sounded.

All at once, the clear notes of Papageno's panpipes rang high above the joyful clamor, and out from the trees skipped the birdman, hand in hand with Papagena, eager to join in the celebrations. Tamino and Pamina, bathed in the warm sunlight, knew that this was the start of their new and happy life together.

 Selection 16

"California is a Garden of Eden, / A paradise to live in or see. / But believe it or not you won't find it so hot, / If you ain't got the do-re-mi."

UTAH

COLO

Los Angeles

ROUTE 66

CALIFORNIA BORDER PATROL

OUT OF GAS

CALIFORNIA

ARIZONA

NEW

PACIFIC OCEAN

MEXICO

"We loaded our jalopies / And piled our families in, / We rattled down that highway / To never come back again."

As I was walking that ribbon of highway,
I saw above me that endless skyway;
I saw below me that golden valley;
This land was made for you and me.

[Chorus]

I've roamed and rambled and I followed my footsteps
To the sparkling sands of her diamond deserts;
And all around me a voice was sounding:
This land was made for you and me.

[Chorus]

When the sun came shining, and I was strolling,
And the wheat fields waving and the dust clouds rolling,
As the fog was lifting a voice was chanting:
This land was made for you and me.

[Chorus]

As I went walking, I saw a sign there,
And on the sign it said "No Trespassing."
But on the other side it didn't say nothing;
That side was made for you and me.

[Chorus]

In the shadow of the steeple I saw my people;
By the relief office I seen my people;
As they stood there hungry, I stood there asking,
Is this land made for you and me?

[Chorus]

Nobody living can ever stop me,
As I go walking that freedom highway;
Nobody living can ever make me turn back;
This land was made for you and me.

Note: In the Canadian version, the chorus lyrics "From California ... to the Gulf Stream waters" are replaced by "From Bonavista to Vancouver Island; / From the Arctic Circle to the Great Lake waters." And in the second verse, the lyrics "To the sparkling sands of her diamond deserts" are replaced by "To the fir-clad forests of our mighty mountains." These words were written by the Travellers, a Canadian folk group.

To my kids, Anna and Cole—
Grandpa loves you! —Nora Guthrie

To my father, Frank W. J.
Love you, Pop! —Kathy Jakobsen

Second Edition

"This Land Is Your Land"
Words and music by Woody Guthrie
TRO — © copyright 1956 (renewed), 1958 (renewed), 1970 and 1972 Ludlow Music, Inc., New York, NY. International copyright secured. All rights reserved, including public performance for profit. Used by permission of Ludlow Music, Inc.

"A Tribute to Woody Guthrie" copyright © 1998 by Pete Seeger
Scrapbook text copyright © 1998 by Janelle Yates

This Land Is Your Land disc
Words and Music by Woody Guthrie
All songs © TRO-Ludlow Music, Inc., New York, NY. Used by Permission: This Land Is Your Land, Howdi Do, Jig Along Home, Mail Myself to You
All songs © TRO-Folkways Music Publishers, Inc., New York, NY. Used by permission: Riding In My Car, Bling-Blang, All Work Together, Grassey Grass Grass (Grow, Grow, Grow), So Long It's Been Good To Know Yuh (Dusty Old Dust)

Produced under license from Rounder Records Corp., One Camp Street, Cambridge, Massachusetts, 02140 U.S.A., www.rounder.com

All quotes read left to right, top to bottom are by Woody Guthrie unless otherwise noted. All Woody Guthrie quotes © Woody Guthrie Publications, Inc. Used by permission. Woody Guthrie lyrics used in borders © TRO Ludlow Music Inc. unless otherwise noted. Used by permission.
Endpapers: Do Re Mi, Dust Storm Disaster. p. 6: Going Down the Road (TRO-Hollis Music, Inc.); Pastures of Plenty. p. 7: New York Town, Seamen Three, Over the Waves and Gone Again (Woody Guthrie Publications, Inc.). p. 8: Little Seed (TRO-Folkways Music Publishers, Inc.). p. 9: Howdido. p. 12: Woody and Lefty Lou's Theme Song (Woody Guthrie Publications, Inc.), Talking Subway Blues, Ramblin' 'Round. p. 13: I Ain't Got No Home, Oklahoma Hills (Michael H. Goldsen, Inc.), Hard Travelin'. p. 16: Pastures of Plenty; Tom Joad; So Long, It's Been Good to Know Yuh (TRO-Folkways Music Publishers, Inc.); Union Maid. p. 17: Roll On, Columbia; This Train Is Bound for Glory (Woody Guthrie Publications, Inc.); Dust Can't Kill Me; Pastures of Plenty. p. 21: Biggest Thing That Man Has Ever Done, My Daddy Flies a Ship in the Sky. p. 24: Grassey Grass Grass & Dance Around (TRO-Folkways Music Publishers, Inc.). p. 25: Pretty Boy Floyd (Fall River Music, Inc.)

Library of Congress Cataloging-in-Publication Data
Guthrie, Woody, 1912-1967.
    This land is your land / words and music by Woody Guthrie : paintings by Kathy
Jakobsen ; with a tribute by Pete Seeger — 1st ed.
        p.   cm.
    Includes musical notation
    Summary: This well-known folk song is accompanied by a tribute from folksinger Pete Seeger, the musical notation, and a biographical scrapbook with photographs.
    ISBN 0-316-06564-1
    1. Folk songs, English — United States — Texts.   [1. Folk songs — United States.]   I. Jakobsen, Kathy, ill.   II. Title.
PZ8.3.G9635Th 1998
782.42162'13'00268 — dc21
[E]   96-54628
10 9 8 7 6 5 4 3 2 1   IP

Printed in Singapore

The paintings for this book were done in oil on canvas. The painted borders were inspired by notch carvings found in traditional "tramp art" — boxes, picture frames, and mirror frames crafted by tramps, hoboes, miners, and lumberjacks in the early to mid-1900s. The artist researched Woody Guthrie's life extensively, and the illustrations feature people and places that were important in his life and travels.

For more information about Woody Guthrie, please contact the Woody Guthrie Archives, at 250 West 57th Street, Suite 1218, New York, NY 10107. www.woodyguthrie.org

This Land Is Your Land

Words and Music by Woody Guthrie

"A SONG DON'T HAVE TO BE AS OLD AS THE HILLS TO BE GOOD, TRUE, OR HONEST. SONGS THAT TELL THE TRUE BATTLE OF OUR PEOPLE TO GET BETTER AND BETTER CONDITIONS EVERYWHERE ARE AS GOOD HOT OR COLD, NEW OR OLD, JUST SO'S THEY'RE HONEST."

Courtesy of the Woody Guthrie Archives

Woody entertains some migrant workers.

"LOTS OF SONGS I MAKE UP WHEN I'M LAUGHING AND CELEBRATING MAKE FOLKS CRY, AND SONGS I MAKE UP WHEN I'M FEELING DOWN AND OUT MAKE PEOPLE LAUGH. THESE TWO UPSIDE-DOWN FEELINGS HAS GOT TO BE IN ANY SONG TO MAKE IT TAKE A HOLD AND LAST."

Courtesy of the Woody Guthrie Archives

IN CALIFORNIA, Woody got a job singing on the radio. His show was popular in the migrant camps. After visiting the camps himself, Woody started writing songs about the migrants— their hard luck and their courage.

In 1940, when he was twenty-eight, Woody went to New York City. He sang for factory workers trying to get better working conditions and higher pay. He sang on street corners with new friends like Pete Seeger and Leadbelly. He began to record his songs, including a new one called "This Land Is Your Land." He also wrote a book about his life titled *Bound for Glory*.

When World War II broke out, Woody sailed to Europe with the merchant marine on large ships carrying supplies and soldiers. After the war, he came home and wrote children's songs for his little daughter Cathy and her friends. Kids were some of Woody's favorite audiences.

In 1952, Woody learned he had Huntington's disease. He was forty years old. He wrote, played his guitar, and visited friends and family a few more years, but finally went to live in a hospital.

By the time he died, in 1967, Woody had written more than one thousand songs, including the classics "Deportee," "Pastures of Plenty," and "Roll On, Columbia;" two novels based on his life; and hundreds of stories. Because he always spoke out for people of all colors and races, especially the poor, he inspired many musicians to do the same.

"Stick up for what you know is right," Woody wrote. "This land was made for you and me."

Eric Schaal, *Life Magazine* © Time Inc.

Woody picks guitar for some young fans.

Stephen Deutsch, Chicago Historical Society. Neg. 38902

Woody with his good friend Leadbelly

This land is your land, this land is my land,
From California to the New York island;

Nobody living can ever make me turn back;
This land was made for you and me.

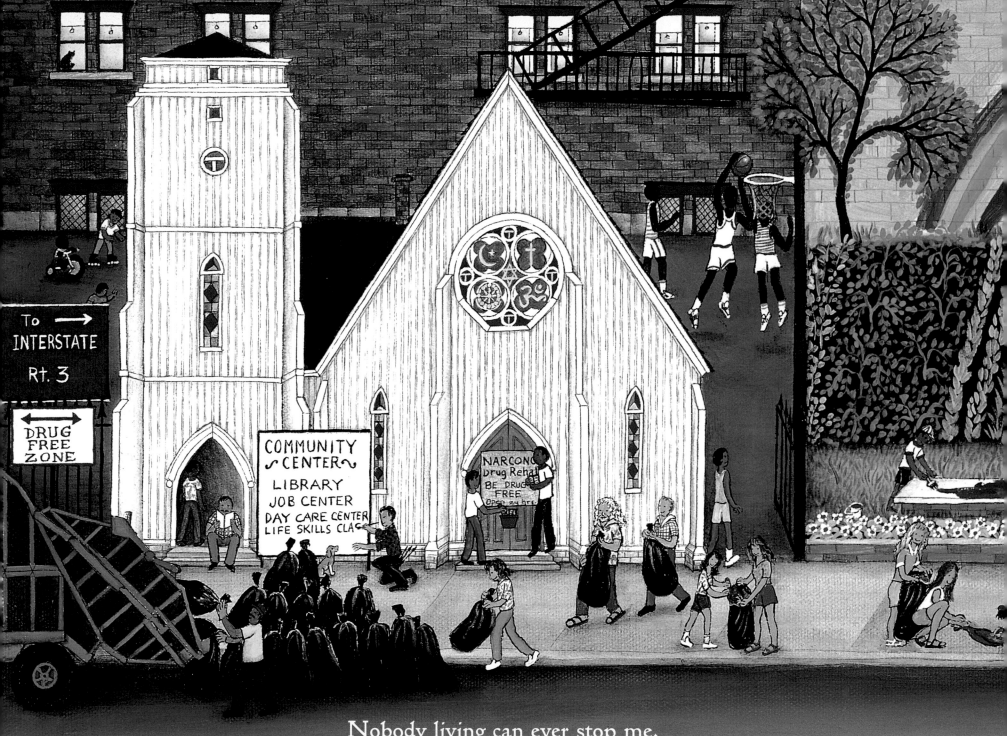

Nobody living can ever stop me,
As I go walking that freedom highway;

Woody Guthrie and friends singing his songs, 1935–1967
Left to right: Woody Guthrie, Leadbelly, Lefty Lou, Cisco Houston, Will Geer, Tom Paxton, Ramblin' Jack Elliott, Lee Hays, Ronnie Gilbert, Pete Seeger, Fred Hellerman, Joan Baez, Arlo Guthrie, Phil Ochs, Odetta, Bob Dylan, Judy Collins, Richie Havens, Peter Yarrow, Mary Travers, Paul Stookey. Seated: Sonny Terry, Brownie McGhee

Woody Guthrie tribute concert, Rock and Roll Hall of Fame, Cleveland 1996
Row 1 (left to right): Paul Metza, Dave Pirner, Emily Saliers, Amy Ray, Dan Bern, David Lutken, James Stein, Mimi Bessette, Lisa Asher, Neil Woodward
Row 2 (left to right): Alejandro Escovedo, David Perales, John Wesley Harding, Jimmy LaFave, Jimmie Dale Gilmore, Syd Straw, Ani DiFranco, Ramblin' Jack Elliott, Pete Seeger, Bruce Springsteen, Arlo Guthrie, Country Joe McDonald, Nora Guthrie, Anna Guthrie Rotante, Billy Bragg, Joe Ely, Jorma Kaukonen, Tim Robbins, Harold Leventhal

This land is your land, this land is my land,
From California to the New York island;

Pete Seeger singing at the Clearwater Festival

CLEARWATER

Marjorie Guthrie's dance class

Boston Pops performing "This Land" at Fourth of July celebration

Watts Towers, Los Angeles

Totem pole, Ketchikan, Alaska

From the redwood forest to the Gulf Stream waters,
This land was made for you and me.

As they stood there hungry, I stood there asking,
Is this land made for you and me?

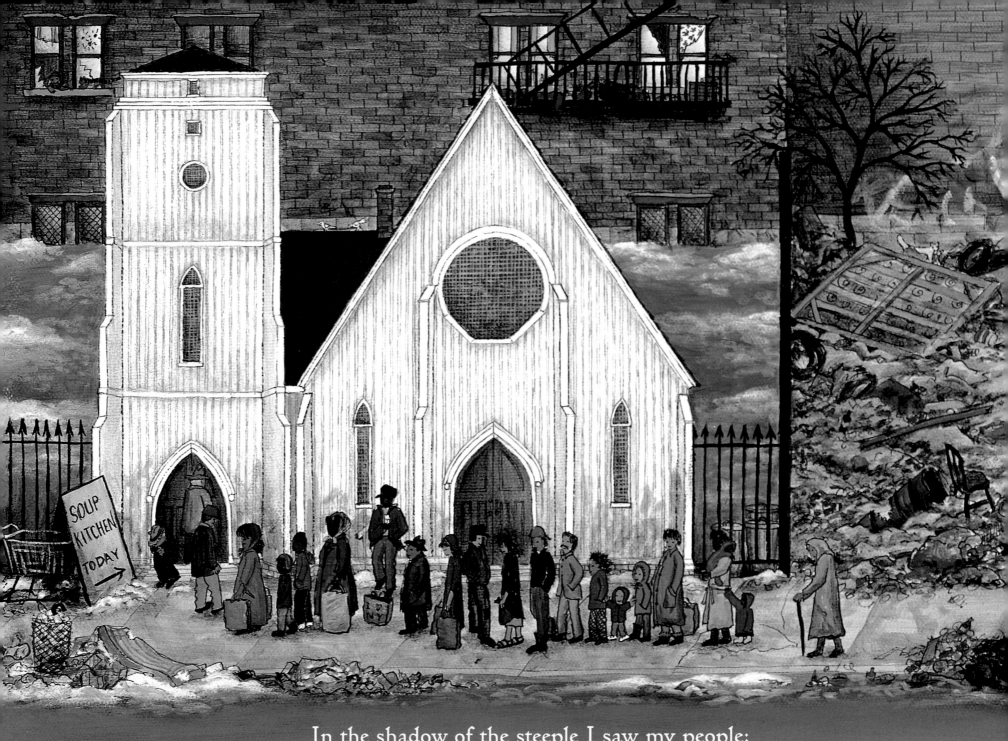

In the shadow of the steeple I saw my people;
By the relief office I seen my people;

From the redwood forest to the Gulf Stream waters,
This land was made for you and me.

"Songs come to me best when walking down the road."

"The people are building a peaceful world, and when the job is done, / That'll be the biggest thing that man has ever done."

Firestone Farm, Greenfield Village, Michigan

Portland Head Light Station, Maine

Woody on the road

Mesa Verde, Colorado

Seattle Space Needle

Oak Alley, Vacherie, Louisiana

Space Shuttle launch, Florida

"So go the new road and see the new things — feel the new way and breathe the new air."

Brooks Range, Alaska

"My daddy rides that ship in the sky. / Mama's not afraid and neither am I."

This land is your land, this land is my land,
From California to the New York island;

"Stick up for what you know is right."

"Let's rake it up and shake it up and go."

Diamond Head and Waikiki Beach, Honolulu

Coney Island Amusement Park

Chinese Theater, Hollywood

Grand Canyon

Coney Island beach

Upper and Lower Yosemite Falls

Washington Monument

"I don't want the kids to be grown up. I want to see the grown-ups be kids."

"If I don't sing when I feel like singing, I go nuts, and stay that way till I do sing."

Crazy Horse Memorial, South Dakota

Mount Rushmore, South Dakota

Stone Mountain Memorial, Georgia

But on the other side it didn't say nothing;
That side was made for you and me.

As I went walking, I saw a sign there,
And on the sign it said "No Trespassing."

**From the redwood forest to the Gulf Stream waters,
This land was made for you and me.**

Grand Coulee Dam construction

Northern train ride

Columbia River, Crown Point, Oregon

Picking peaches

Oil well

Wawona tunnel tree, Yosemite National Park

Dining car train

This land is your land, this land is my land,
From California to the New York island;

"It's a mighty hard row that my poor hands have hoed; / My poor feet have traveled a hot dusty road."

"Wherever men are fightin' for their rights, / That's where I'm gonna be, Ma, / That's where I'm gonna be."

Los Angeles City Hall

Migrant farmworkers

Okemah, Oklahoma

THE GRAPES OF WRATH

CRYSTAL

Woody singing at a migrant camp

Dust Bowl refugees

Garment workers

JOIN the CIO

ON Strike

WORKERS UNITE

Water tower, Chicago

"So long, it's been good to know ye, / This dusty old dust is a getting my home, / And I've got to be drifting along."

Hobo train

$00 $INE

SHIP AND TRAVEL Santa Fe all the way

"Oh you can't scare me, / I'm sticking to the union. / I'm sticking to the union / till the day I die."

As the fog was lifting a voice was chanting:
This land was made for you and me.

When the sun came shining, and I was strolling,
And the wheat fields waving and the dust clouds rolling,

From the redwood forest to the Gulf Stream waters,
This land was made for you and me.

"I mined in your mines / And I gathered in your corn; / been working, mister, / Since the day that I was born."

"Some days I'm wild / Some nights I'm tame / But no two minutes / Am I the same."

Iowa cornfield

Shrimp fishing, Gulf of Mexico

Woody's cowboy band, Pampa, Texas

California redwoods

Rodeo

Mardi Gras, New Orleans

"General Grant," giant sequoia, California

"Way down yonder in the Indian nation / I ride my pony on the reservation / In those Oklahoma hills where I was born."

"I've been having some hard traveling, / I thought you knowed . . . / I've been a-working that Pittsburgh steel."

Mississippi River

Delta Queen

Gateway Arch, St. Louis, Missouri

This land is your land, this land is my land,
From California to the New York island;

"Drop whatever you are doing, / Stop your work and worry, too; / Sit right down and take it easy, / Here comes Woody and Lefty Lou."

"I blowed into New York town. / I looked up and I looked down. / Everybody I seen on the street / Was all a-runnin' down a hole in the ground."

Hollywood Hills

KFVD

HOLLYWOOD

SUBWAY

New York City

San Francisco

Niagara Falls

Homeless people camped out under bridge

California beach

Empire State Building

"I'm out to do the best I can / As I go ramblin' around."

Brooklyn Bridge

"I hate a song that makes you think you are just born to lose."

And all around me a voice was sounding:
This land was made for you and me.

I've roamed and rambled and I followed my footsteps
To the sparkling sands of her diamond deserts;

"I stick out my little hand / To ev'ry woman, kid and man / And I shake it up and down, / Howjido, howjido."

"On my sidewalk, on my street, / Any place that we do meet, / Then I'll shake you by your hand, / Howjido, howjido."

"I feel glad when you feel good, / I brighten up my neighborhood, / Shakin' hands with ev'rybody, / Howjido, howjido."

"When I meet a dog or cat, / I will rubby rub his back, / Shakey, shakey, shakey paw, / Howjido, howjido."

From the redwood forest to the Gulf Stream waters,
This land was made for you and me.

"We'll all dance around and see my little seed grow."

"The sun got hot and my ground got dry. / I thought my little seed would burn and die."

"The rain it come and it washed my ground. / I thought my little seed was going to drown."

"The snow it blowed and the wind it blew; / My little seed grew and it grew and it grew."

"I was standing
...own in New York
...one day, / ...ng hey, hey,
hey."

"We were seamen
three, / Cisco,
Jimmy, and me; /
Keep a-fightin' and
a-singin' / Till the
world gets free /
Across our lands
and seas."

...York Town,
...York City, /
...York Street,
...York
...thing, / N.Y.
...Y. N.Y. N.Y.

"Our cargo it was
TNT. / Our ship
she was the
William Bee. /
Over the waves
and gone again. /
Over the waves
and gone."

This land is your land, this land is my land,
From California to the New York island;

"Left wing, chicken wing, it's all the same to me."

Woody...
favorite f...

"I'm goin' where the climate suits my clothes. . . . / I'm goin' where them grapes an' peaches grow."

"My land I'll defend with... life, if it be... 'Cause my pe... tures of plen... must always... free."

This land was made for you and me.

I saw below me that golden valley;

I saw above me that endless skyway;

As I was walking that ribbon of highway,

Your Land

PETE SEEGER

Paintings by Kathy Jakobsen

Megan Tingley Books

Little, Brown and Company
BOSTON NEW YORK LONDON

A Note from Nora Guthrie

When we decided to publish a picture book based on my father's song "This Land Is Your Land," we all knew that the project would be a challenge, because the song represents so many aspects of our American history and culture. It is often the first song children learn in music class at school, and it is sung at protest rallies and community gatherings throughout the country.

When artist Kathy Jakobsen first came to the Woody Guthrie Archives to research the illustrations for this project, she collected every book and recording she could carry. Almost a year later, she came by with pages of notes, sketches, and questions. "Do you know what kind of fence Woody's childhood house had?" she asked. "Do you have any photographs of Woody's mother, so I can see what kind of dress she wore?" "Do you know if the road went this way, straight or curved?" I realized that day that she had been quietly reading, listening, investigating, and researching not only the story of the song itself, but Woody's whole life. She uncovered hundreds of minuscule details and facts and wove them together into a tapestry of his life, his music, his politics, his travels, his family, and his ideas, hopes, and dreams. The beautiful paintings she created draw meaning from specific moments in both Woody's and the country's lives. Side by side, images of lush fruit groves co-exist with images of people lined up at a relief office, giving us the full breadth of our national experience. The idea behind "This Land Is Your Land" seems to be an ongoing dialogue. I like to think that everyone who sees this book shares our experience of family, history, and the multifaceted concept of citizenship.

This beautiful book offers children a chance to read and consider Woody's words, but we also wanted them to be able to hear his voice and sing along, so we have now added a compact disc to accompany the book. The songs included on the compact disc were specially selected to complement the scenes portrayed in the book, and some of the lyrics appear in the borders throughout. Although I grew up on these songs, it wasn't until I had kids of my own that I came to appreciate my dad's genius for finding just the right way to tap into a kid's mind. I also realized how closely he had been watching us! He watched our movements and gestures, "Howdi Do," he listened to our words, "Grassey Grass Grass," he encouraged our ideas, "Mail Myself to You," and he heard our feelings, "Riding in My Car." Knowing how to speak our language, he was also able to use his songs to get some necessary things done! Parenting, for my dad, often came in a rhyme or a melody. The challenge of keeping the house clean became "All Work Together." A lesson in how to cooperate on a project (without fighting!) became "Bling-Blang." Whatever needs came up as situations arose, a song came out. Our daily lives and development were forever documented in the hundreds of children's songs he left us with.

In 2002 we celebrate what would have been my father's ninetieth year. What better way to celebrate his birthday than by giving you, his fans and friends, a gift!

Woody as a baby with his sister, Clara

Courtesy of the Woody Guthrie Archives

WOODY GUTHRIE was born on July 14,

1912, in the dusty little town of Okemah, Oklahoma. Charley and Nora Guthrie named their son Woodrow Wilson, but everybody called him "plain old Woody."

When Woody was six, his family started having some hard luck. Their new house burned down, and a few years later, Woody's sister died in a fire. His mother got sick and had to live in a hospital.

When Woody was seventeen, he moved to Texas. In flat, windy Pampa, he found an old guitar and learned to play. He liked to sing ballads — long songs that tell a story. He formed a band with some friends and started writing songs about his experiences and the folks he met along the way.

In 1929, people everywhere faced hard times. They called this period the Great Depression. In Texas, it stopped raining. Fierce winds piled dust over the land. The farms around Pampa "dried up and blowed away." Someone said it looked like a big dust bowl. And it did.

Lots of folks in that Dust Bowl packed up and headed for California, looking for jobs and new homes. Woody headed west, too, hitching rides and hopping freight trains when he could. California was filling up with people from Oklahoma, Texas, and other states. These travelers were called migrants or "Okies."

The migrants ended up in crowded camps. Their "homes" were tents and small rooms pieced together from scraps. And there weren't enough jobs to go around.

The Guthrie family on their porch in Okemah

"MY EYES HAS BEEN MY CAMERA TAKING PICTURES OF THE WORLD AND MY SONGS HAS BEEN MESSAGES THAT I TRIED TO SCATTER ACROSS THE BACK SIDES AND ALONG THE STEPS OF THE FIRE ESCAPES AND ON THE WINDOWSILLS AND THROUGH THE DARK HALLS."

Courtesy of the Dorothea Lange Collection, the Oakland Museum. Gift of Paul S. Taylor.

One of many families on the road to California

Woody's band in Pampa, Texas. He is the first "cowboy" on the left.

From the redwood forest to the Gulf Stream waters,

A Tribute to
WOODY GUTHRIE

Woody and Pete Seeger at one of the many concerts they played together

"A FOLK SONG IS WHAT'S WRONG AND HOW TO FIX IT OR
IT COULD BE WHO'S HUNGRY AND WHERE THEIR MOUTH
IS OR WHO'S OUT OF WORK AND WHERE THE JOB IS OR
WHO'S BROKE AND WHERE THE MONEY IS OR WHO'S
CARRYING A GUN AND WHERE THE PEACE IS."
— WOODY GUTHRIE

I first heard "This Land Is Your Land" on the Folkways recording, 1949. My first reaction was "It's a nice idea, but the tune is too simple. This song is one of Woody's lesser efforts."

That shows how wrong you can be. Over the years I've realized that it's easy to get complicated. But Woody had a genius for simplicity. This song now has reached hundreds of millions of people.

Maybe billions of people.

The song was never on the Top 40, but it got into schools and summer camps. It went from one guitar picker to another. I now get audiences singing every verse without needing any songbooks, because I call out the words to them line by line without losing the rhythm.

When some high voices can add harmony, like two notes above the melody, then we get hope for the future of the human race.

Woody wrote the song in the windy, icy February of 19 and 40, when he hitchhiked from Los Angeles to New York City. The original fourth line of each verse then was "God blessed America for me." (Irving Berlin's famous song, sung by Kate Smith, was on all the jukeboxes in the roadside diners at that time.)

I never heard Woody sing it till 1949, when he recorded it for the tiny Folkways Recording Company with the fourth line we all know now.

He wrote thousands of songs. The 1949 recording of "This Land," and later the school songbooks, omitted some of the best verses. Nowadays Arlo Guthrie and I and many others make sure to include them. Because it's important to remember that if the sign says "No Trespassing" on one side, on the other side "It didn't say nothing. That side was made for you and me."

Somewhere Woody is grinning and saying to us all, "Take it easy, but take it!"

— PETE SEEGER, 1998

This land was made for you and me.